Lucy on the Loose

by Ilene Cooper
illustrated by Amanda Harvey

A STEPPING STONE BOOK™
Random House 🏠 New York

For Bill—and for Lucy, Jet, Mitzi,
and all the other dogs of Dallas
—I.C.

To Angelise
—A.H.

Text copyright © 2000 by Ilene Cooper
Interior illustrations copyright © 2000 by Amanda Harvey
Cover illustration copyright © 2007 by Mary Ann Lasher

www.steppingstonesbooks.com
www.randomhouse.com/kids

Educators and librarians, for a variety of teaching tools, visit us at
www.randomhouse.com/teachers

Library of Congress Cataloging-in-Publication Data
Cooper, Ilene.
Lucy on the loose / by Ilene Cooper ; illustrated by Amanda Harvey.
    p.   cm. — "A Stepping Stone book."
SUMMARY: When his beagle Lucy runs off chasing a big orange cat, Bobby must overcome his shyness in order to find them again.
ISBN 978-0-307-26508-1 (pbk.) — ISBN 978-0-307-46508-5 (lib. bdg.)
[1. Beagle (Dog breed)—Fiction. 2. Dogs—Fiction. 3. Cats—Fiction.
4. Lost and found possessions—Fiction. 5. Bashfulness—Fiction.]
I. Harvey, Amanda, ill. II. Title.
PZ7.C7856Lu 2007   [Fic]—dc22   2006021379

Printed in the United States of America   12 11 10 9 8 7 6 5 4 3 2 1

Contents

1
Who's That Cat?

Lucy was Bobby Quinn's dog. She was a great dog!

She was a beagle. She was white and brown with black spots. Her eyes were soft and dark, like chocolate candy.

Lucy liked to jump. She liked to run. She loved to run! Lucy loved running up to people. She thought everyone was her friend.

Bobby was shy. Meeting new people made his heart pound fast. His face got red. Even his ears got red.

But Bobby wasn't so shy when he was with Lucy. She helped Bobby make friends. Shawn was a friend Bobby had made, thanks to Lucy.

Shawn was a new boy in the neighborhood. He had just moved in that summer. At first, Bobby was afraid to go across the street and say hello. But Lucy wasn't. And she pulled Bobby right along with her.

Shawn was shy, too, just like Bobby. But Bobby and Shawn weren't shy with each other. They played ball. They drew cartoons. And they spent lots of time chasing Lucy.

Lucy loved to run in circles around Bobby's big yard. The boys tried to catch her. Lucy tried to get away.

Fast Lucy slipped between their legs.

Slippery Lucy wiggled out of their grasp.

Then she'd run around some more.

Bobby and Shawn just laughed. It was hard to keep up with Lucy.

One day, Shawn came over to Bobby's house. Bobby was swinging in the hammock. Lucy was curled up at his feet. Summer was almost over, but it was still hot.

"Hey, Bobby. Hey, Lucy," Shawn said.

"Hi, Shawn," Bobby greeted his friend. Lucy gave a happy bark.

"Want to go get some comic books?" Shawn asked.

Bobby sat up. Lucy sat up, too. "Absolutely," he said. Absolutely was Bobby's favorite word.

Bobby liked to draw. He used comic books to practice drawing his own superheroes.

Bobby ran inside. He asked his mother

if he could go with Shawn to the Buy Lo store on Main Street.

"I really, really need some new comics," Bobby told his mother.

Mrs. Quinn laughed. "Oh, really? Then I guess you can go."

"And can I take Lucy?" he asked.

"All right," Mrs. Quinn said. "But hold onto her. You know how Lucy likes to tug on her leash."

"Okay," Bobby said. He thought his mother worried too much. He knew how to take care of Lucy.

Mrs. Quinn gave Bobby some money for comics. Bobby raced back outside.

Lucy was standing with her paws on the fence. She was barking short, hard barks.

"What's wrong?" Bobby asked Shawn.

"A cat," Shawn said.

"What cat?"

Shawn pointed. On the sidewalk was a big orange cat. A huge orange cat. The cat was licking his paws and swinging his long tail. The cat ignored Lucy. Lucy barked harder.

"Calm down, Lucy," Bobby said. "That cat's not bothering you." Bobby led Lucy away from the fence. He patted Lucy's head as he snapped on her leash.

Lucy's warm tongue gave Bobby's hand a lick.

But her eyes were on that big orange cat.

2
Comic Books

Bobby, Shawn, and Lucy walked past the big yellow house on the corner. It was where Mr. Davis lived.

Mr. Davis was another friend Bobby had made with Lucy's help.

Bobby used to be scared of Mr. Davis. He thought that maybe Mr. Davis was a grumpy old man. But Mr. Davis was nice. He liked puttering around his garden.

"Hi, boys," he said. He clipped a rose from the rosebush. Lucy barked hello.

"There's my gal," Mr. Davis said.

"We're going to get comic books," Bobby told him.

"Mind if I come?" Mr. Davis asked. "I could use the exercise."

Mr. Davis walked slowly, but Shawn and Bobby didn't mind. Mr. Davis always had interesting stories to tell.

Today he told the boys about growing up listening to radio shows. There was no television when he was a boy. Bobby and Shawn couldn't imagine a time without television. Even Lucy liked to watch TV if there were dogs on.

"Oh, there were great shows," Mr. Davis said. "The Lone Ranger was my favorite. He was a cowboy. Wore a black mask over his eyes. And he rode a horse named Silver."

"The Lone Ranger," Bobby said softly. He liked the sound of that. The Lone Ranger and Silver might be fun to draw.

Main Street was only two short blocks from Mr. Davis's house. "Where do you buy your comics?" Mr. Davis asked when they got to the corner of Main and First.

"Right here at Buy Lo," Bobby said.

"Why don't I wait outside with Lucy?" Mr. Davis suggested. Lucy yipped. She seemed to like the idea.

Mr. Davis sat down on a bench in front of the store. Lucy got busy sniffing the feet of the people who walked by.

The boys went in the Buy Lo. It sold all sorts of things from lipsticks to notebook paper. It was a big store, but it wasn't very busy today. Bobby and Shawn hurried to the aisle where the comics were kept.

"Hey!" Shawn exclaimed. "They're not here."

A rack of ladies' stockings stood where

the comics used to be. Bobby looked around. "It looks like they moved a bunch of stuff."

"Why did they have to do that?" Shawn muttered.

"Let's check out the other aisles," Bobby said. "Maybe we'll find them."

The boys walked up one aisle. They walked down another.

No comic books.

The boys looked at each other. "Now what?" Shawn said.

"I suppose we could ask someone," Bobby answered slowly.

Maybe Bobby was not as shy as he used to be, but talking to a salesperson still seemed hard.

"Naw," Shawn said, "we can find them on our own. Let's look around more."

Toothpaste. Brushes. Bags of candy.

No comics.

Magazines. Paper towels. Tummy medicine.

No comics.

"Stupid store," Shawn muttered.

A man wearing a name tag pinned to his bright blue jacket walked by. He worked in the store.

Should I stop him? Bobby wondered. Bobby felt his stomach go up and down. The rest of him didn't make a move.

"He looked busy," Bobby murmured.

"Yeah," Shawn agreed.

Both boys were glum.

"I guess they don't sell comic books anymore," Bobby said.

"Stupid store," Shawn repeated.

The boys trudged toward the door.

They were just about to leave when Bobby cried, "Hey, look!"

There was a big wire rack filled with comics next to the checkout counter.

Bobby and Shawn ran over to the rack. Bobby picked out a Spiderman comic. Shawn took a Superman comic. "Brand-new ones," Shawn said happily. "This store is okay!"

The boys went outside. Mr. Davis and Lucy were waiting.

"That took a while," Mr. Davis said. "Did you find the comics you were looking for?"

"Yes," Bobby said. He and Shawn looked at each other. They were thinking the same thing.

They almost didn't find the comics at all because they were too shy to ask.

3
Lucy on the Loose

"Mom, can Lucy and I go over to Shawn's?" Bobby asked the next day.

Mrs. Quinn was settled down in the living room. She was enjoying her morning cup of coffee and her newspaper.

"All right," she said. "But be sure to keep Lucy on her leash. Shawn's house doesn't have a fence, you know."

Bobby knew. His mother reminded him about that every time he took Lucy to Shawn's. She really did worry too much.

Bobby pulled Lucy's leash out of his pocket and clipped it to her collar.

They had just crossed the street when

Lucy jerked to a stop. She stood still. Her nose quivered.

"What is it, girl?" Bobby asked.

Lucy started to bark. She jumped up on her hind legs. Bobby looked to where Lucy was pointing with her nose.

"I knew it!" he muttered. The cat was behind a big fir tree.

Lucy tugged and pulled. Bobby held her leash tight.

"C'mon, Lucy," Bobby told her. "Just ignore that old cat. We're going to Shawn's."

Lucy followed Bobby as he pulled her along. But she kept looking back.

Bobby glanced back, too. He knew cats couldn't smile. But this cat looked like he was grinning right at them.

"I'm still here," the cat seemed to say. "What are you going to do about it?"

Bobby forgot about the cat as soon as he got to Shawn's house. Shawn was sitting on the front steps. He was reading his new Superman comic.

Bobby plunked down on the step next to Shawn. "Is it good?" he asked.

"It's great!" Shawn said.

Shawn's little brother came up to the boys. "I want to look, too!" said Ben.

Ben always wanted to do everything Bobby and Shawn were doing.

"Ben, go away," Shawn said.

Shawn had an older sister and a younger brother. Bobby didn't have any brothers or sisters. He thought Shawn was being a little mean. "Ben, maybe there's a good show on TV," Bobby suggested.

"Yeah, Ben, go inside and watch TV," Shawn said.

"No. N-O," said Ben.

Ben was starting kindergarten in the fall. But he was already learning to spell.

Shawn shook his head. "All right, stay. But you can't look at the comic book."

Ben stuck out his lower lip. He plopped down on the grass next to Lucy.

Lucy tried to make Ben feel better. She licked his cheek. Ben petted Lucy's back.

"That's good, Ben," Bobby said. "You can play with Lucy."

"Lucy is a D-O-G," Ben spelled.

Bobby laughed. "Right. D-O-G spells dog. L-U-C-Y spells Lucy."

Ben repeated the letters carefully. "L-U-C-Y."

"Oh, don't encourage him," Shawn said. "He spells all the time. He's driving everybody crazy."

Bobby looked down at the comic book. "What's this one about?" he asked Shawn.

"Superman is trying to save an airplane," Shawn told him. "It's going to crash. See?" Shawn pointed at one of the pictures. "He's keeping the airplane in the air. With one hand."

"Cool!" Bobby said. He started reading the comic book over Shawn's shoulder. "You know, I could draw a Superman comic strip."

"Yeah?" Shawn looked impressed.

"Absolutely," Bobby said.

"I've got some paper and markers in the house," Shawn said.

"We can make up a comic strip for the Lone Ranger, too," Bobby said.

"That's a great idea," Shawn said. "Maybe Superman and the Lone Ranger could join forces." He jumped up. "I'll be right back with the stuff," Shawn called as he ran into the house.

Bobby started thinking about an adventure for the Lone Ranger and Superman. Maybe he could put Lucy in the comic strip, too.

Lucy! Where was she?

Bobby looked around for Lucy. She was playing with Ben.

Ben tossed a stick. Lucy brought it back. Just like she learned in obedience school.

"Having fun, Ben?" Bobby called.

Ben nodded. "Yep. Does Lucy catch frisbees?"

"Not yet. But we can teach her someday," Bobby said. "She loves to run and catch stuff."

Shawn brought out the markers and paper. Bobby and Shawn spread out over the steps. They started drawing.

Shawn drew Superman flying through the air. Bobby drew the Lone Ranger on his horse, Silver.

"Drawing a horse isn't that easy," Bobby grumbled.

Shawn looked over at Bobby's drawing and chuckled. "Silver looks more like a cow."

Bobby had to laugh, too. "Yeah, I guess he does, kind of."

Just then Ben came running up to the boys.

"Bob-by," Ben stammered.

"What's wrong?" Bobby asked. He looked around. "Hey! Where's Lucy?"

Ben looked scared.

"Ben!" Shawn said. "What happened to Lucy?"

"She . . . she ran away!" Ben said in a shaky voice.

Bobby jumped up. "Lucy ran away? Where?"

"That way." Ben was confused. He pointed in one direction. "Or maybe that way." He pointed in the other direction.

"Which way was it?" Shawn demanded.

"I'm not sure." Ben was almost crying. "But she was chasing a big orange C-A-T!"

4
Looking for Lucy

Lucy was gone.

For a few seconds, Bobby just stood there, not knowing what to do. Even though it was hot, he could feel a cold sweat on his forehead.

Bobby asked Ben, "Are you sure you don't know where Lucy went?"

"Think, Ben," Shawn said.

Ben looked like he might cry. "I was getting a bigger stick. Then I looked up. Lucy was chasing the cat. They ran behind the house, and I ran to get you."

"Maybe she hasn't left the yard yet," Shawn suggested.

"Yeah!" Bobby said.

He started running around the house. Shawn was behind him. Ben was right behind Shawn.

They looked in the backyard. They looked behind the garage. No Lucy. But Shawn did find her leash.

Shawn held it up. "Ben, did you take off Lucy's leash?"

Ben nodded slowly. "It made it hard for her to fetch the stick. She kept tripping on it."

Now Bobby was even more worried. *Without her leash flapping, it will be easier for Lucy to run,* he thought.

"That was dumb," Shawn told Ben.

Tears started to roll down Ben's cheeks.

"What should we do?" Bobby asked. He felt like he might start crying, too.

"Maybe Lucy chased the cat back to your house," Shawn said.

"Maybe," Bobby said. He felt his hopes rise a little.

"Let's go," said Shawn.

Ben tried to follow them.

"No, Ben. You stay here," Shawn told him.

"I don't want to." Ben wiped his eyes with the back of his hand.

"Please wait here, Ben," Bobby said. "Maybe Lucy will come back. Somebody has to be here."

"That'll be your job, Ben," Shawn told him. "Take her leash."

Ben finally nodded. He took the leash. "Okay. I'll wait here. I'll wait for Lucy."

The boys ran across the street to Bobby's house.

"Don't let my mother see us," Bobby whispered to Shawn. "She'll ask where Lucy is."

He peeked in the window. Mrs. Quinn was still inside the house reading the newspaper. Should he tell her about Lucy? No. They might find her any minute and then he wouldn't have to.

Bobby and Shawn searched around the house for Lucy. Maybe she had gotten tired of chasing the cat. Maybe she was resting in one of her favorite spots.

But she was not in the garden. She was not under the shady oak tree.

Bobby felt like a small boat was in the middle of his stomach, rocking up and down.

"Now where?" Shawn whispered.

Bobby tried to think. "Let's check the

park. Maybe Lucy chased the cat there."

There was a small park on the next block. It was mostly for little kids. But today, a couple of big kids were kicking a soccer ball around.

"You could ask them," Shawn said, scuffing the dirt with his feet.

Bobby nodded. But he didn't say anything.

The ball rolled in their direction.

"Hey, kick it over here," one of the kids said.

Bobby kicked the ball.

"Thanks," the kid said. He turned back to the game.

Bobby was shy with most people. But he was really shy around bigger kids. He had to ask, though.

"Hey!" he called.

The kid turned around. He frowned. "What?"

"Did you see a beagle chasing a cat?" Bobby said the words quickly before he could think about them.

The older boy looked surprised. "Yeah."

Bobby took a deep breath. "She's my dog. Where did she go?"

The boy pointed in the direction of Main Street.

This news made Bobby feel really scared. Even more scared than talking to a big kid.

Main Street was a busy place on Saturday. There was noise. There was traffic. It was absolutely no place for a dog on her own.

5
Back to the Buy Lo

The boys rushed downtown. Now they stood on the corner of Main and First. They looked up and down the street. They didn't see Lucy.

"Where do we start?" Shawn asked.

"I don't know," Bobby said helplessly.

"Maybe we should ask around," said Shawn.

"We have to do something," Bobby answered.

Shawn looked in the window of the Buy Lo. "Hey, Bobby, come here. Look how busy the store is."

The store was full of people today.

Some were plucking items off the shelves and putting them in their baskets. Other shoppers were standing in line to pay.

"Lucy wouldn't chase a cat into a store," Bobby said.

"No," Shawn said, "but there are lots of customers in there. Maybe one of them saw Lucy. Of course," Shawn said more slowly, "that's a lot of people to ask."

"Wait a minute!" Bobby exclaimed. "We don't have to ask them all. There's a loudspeaker in the store. I've heard it. We just have to ask the clerk to make an announcement. Everyone in the store will hear it."

The boys hurried into the store.

Bobby looked over at the checkout counter. A friendly-looking lady was at the cash register. She was busy ringing up customers. There was a long line. It would be hard to interrupt her.

But Bobby had to do it. He had to do it for Lucy. He walked up to the woman.

"Excuse me," Bobby said very softly.

The cashier didn't hear him.

"Excuse me," Bobby said more loudly.

The woman looked down at him. "Yes?"

"Hey!" A grouchy man was waiting at the counter. "Get in line!"

"But . . . but . . ." Bobby stammered.

"Is something the matter?" the cashier asked.

"I'm-looking-for-my-dog." Bobby said it all in one breath. "She's lost."

Several people heard Bobby. "Lost dog, lost dog." The news went up and down the checkout line.

"Could you make an announcement? The kind that everyone in the store can hear?" Bobby asked the cashier.

"I suppose," the cashier said. "Tell me what your dog looks like."

"Be quick about it," the grouchy man added.

Bobby tried not to look at all those grown-ups waiting in line. He turned toward the cashier. But he could feel his cheeks getting red anyway.

"Her name is Lucy. She's a beagle, white and brown with black spots. She was chasing an orange cat. They were running toward Main Street." *Whew!*

"Is she wearing a collar?" asked a teenager.

"Yes," Bobby said. "Her name and phone number are on her collar."

The cashier picked up a microphone and clicked it on.

"Shoppers!" she said. "Please be on the lookout around town for a brown and white beagle named Lucy."

Bobby tugged on the woman's sleeve. "She has black spots, too," he whispered.

"A brown and white beagle with black spots," the woman added. "She's lost and was last seen chasing an orange cat. Her name and phone number are on her collar."

"Thank you," Bobby said. "Thanks a lot."

"No problem," the cashier said, "but now I have to get back to work."

Bobby had felt happy when he heard the announcement. But no one in the store came up to them and said they had seen Lucy. He and Shawn were going to have to keep looking.

"You'll find her," the teenager said.

"Have you checked the butcher shop?" asked a woman. "Dogs like bones, you know."

Even the grouchy man called, "Good luck" as the boys went out the door.

"Now what?" Shawn asked.

Bobby shook his head. He was feeling low. "I guess we could try the butcher shop like that lady said."

Shawn shrugged. "Can't hurt. It's right across the street."

Bobby told himself not to worry. There were still lots of places to look for Lucy.

But he couldn't help it. He was worried anyway.

6
Mrs. Agatha Adams

The boys waited at the light to cross the street. Shawn said, "Maybe we should tell your mother about Lucy. She could drive us around town."

Bobby thought about telling her Lucy was lost. He could hear his mother saying, "Keep Lucy on her leash. Shawn's yard doesn't have a fence."

Bobby sighed. She would say he was careless. She'd be mad. Bobby couldn't blame her. He was mad at himself.

"Let's just check out the butcher shop," Bobby said. "Then I'll call home and tell my mother about Lucy."

They were about to enter the store when a familiar voice stopped them. "Hey, you're going in the wrong place. The ice cream shop is next door."

The boys turned around. There was Bobby's friend Candy, licking away at a chocolate ice cream cone.

Candy was another new friend of Bobby's. They met at dog obedience school. Candy's dog, Butch, was the worst dog in the class.

If the teacher said "sit," Butch stood. If the teacher said "fetch," Butch lay down. He flunked the class.

Candy didn't mind. She liked Butch as much as Bobby liked Lucy. Candy liked something else. She liked to talk! She liked to talk as much as Lucy liked to run.

She started talking now. "Hey, Shawn,

remember me? I met you at Bobby's house. It was right after I got back from the lake. I still have my suntan. But it's peeling now." Candy flicked a piece of dead skin off her arm.

"Shawn," she went on, "did you get a dog? You said you might. I was thinking. Maybe you should get a poodle. I almost got a poodle." Candy glanced at Butch. "Poodles are smart. I love Butch, but he's not all that smart. I think Lucy would like to be friends with a poodle. . . ."

"Candy," Bobby interrupted, "Lucy is missing."

"What! When?" Candy sputtered. For once she let Bobby do the talking. Quickly, Bobby told Candy about Lucy and the big orange cat.

"Oh, no!" Candy said. "We have to find

her. Butch and I will help you look." Butch barked loudly and pulled on his leash.

"We're going to ask in here," Bobby said, pointing at the butcher shop. He looked at Butch. "Maybe you should stay out here with Butch."

Candy nodded. "He'd go crazy trying to get at the hamburger meat." She took hold of Butch's leash with both hands.

The boys went into the store. A large man with a black mustache stood behind the counter. He was wearing a white apron and a small white cap on his head.

Inside the glass cases were chops, roasts, and hamburger meat.

"Have you ever been in here before?" Shawn whispered to Bobby.

"Once or twice with my mother," Bobby whispered back. "The man behind

the counter is named Joe. He's nice."

Joe was chopping meat with a huge meat cleaver. *Whack!*

Bobby cleared his throat. "Excuse me."

Joe peered over the counter. "Sorry, I didn't see you. What do you need?"

"I'm looking for my dog," Bobby mumbled.

"Hot dogs, you say?" *Whack!* "I have hot dogs in packages." Joe jerked his thumb toward a cooler. "Over there."

Nervously, Bobby tried again. "Not hot dogs. A regular dog. With four legs."

Now Joe stared down at Bobby. "A dog! I couldn't have a dog in here! The health department would shut me down."

Shawn pulled on Bobby's arm. "Let's just go," he whispered.

"Can't," Bobby whispered back. "My

dog is lost," he continued in a louder voice. "Did you see her?"

Joe stopped whacking. "What does she look like?"

Quickly, Bobby told Joe that Lucy was a white and brown and black beagle with chocolate brown eyes and soft floppy ears.

"She sounds pretty," Joe said.

"She is," Bobby answered. Just thinking about how pretty Lucy was made Bobby feel like crying again.

"Well, I haven't seen her," Joe said. "But sometimes dogs come sniffing around back." Then he put his meat cleaver down. "Wait a minute."

He wiped his hands on his apron. He went to the refrigerator and pulled out some cooked ribs. He dropped them in a paper sack.

"All the dogs like my rib bones," Joe said. "Take them with you. Maybe Lucy will smell them and find you."

Just then, a customer walked into Joe's butcher shop. She was a big woman. She was wearing an orange dress and a little hat. Her hair was a funny color. It was almost as orange as her dress.

"I'll be with you in a moment," Joe said to her. He handed Bobby the rib bones. "Good luck finding your dog."

The woman with the orange hair looked at Bobby. "Is your dog lost?"

Bobby nodded.

"You poor boy. The same thing happened to me. My cat ran away. She's been gone three days. I feel terrible about it. Terrible. Terrible." The lady with the orange hair shook her head.

Bobby had a thought. "What does your cat look like?" he asked.

"My cat is beautiful," the woman said with a sniff. "He's quite large. He has a long fluffy tail. He's a special color, too."

"What color?" Bobby asked.

The woman patted her hair. "Very much like the color of my hair."

"Orange!" Bobby said with excitement.

The woman frowned. "I would not call my hair orange. It is ginger. And that's my cat's name. Ginger."

Bobby and Shawn looked at each other.

"The last time anyone saw my dog she was chasing a cat," Bobby said. "It was big and—" Bobby almost said orange.

"It was big and ginger."

7
The Parade

"Ginger!" the lady cried. "You've seen her?"

"I think so," Bobby said.

The lady forgot about buying anything. She hustled Shawn and Bobby out of the butcher shop.

"We must find Ginger," she told them. "It's been three days."

Candy was still licking her ice cream cone. She was confused.

"Who is Ginger?" she whispered to Bobby. "And who is that woman?"

The woman heard her. She pulled herself up to her full height. "I am Mrs.

Agatha Adams," she said. She pointed at Bobby. "And his dog is chasing my sweet cat, Ginger!"

Candy turned to Bobby. "I just saw a friend from camp. I told her about Lucy running away. My friend said she saw a beagle chasing a cat near the fire station."

"Wow!" Shawn said. "Let's go."

Bobby jogged toward the fire station. Shawn was right behind him, holding the bag of bones for Lucy. His shoelaces were flapping, but he didn't stop to tie them. Mrs. Agatha Adams was huffing and puffing behind Shawn. She clutched her tiny hat. Butch pranced next to Mrs. Adams. Candy brought up the rear. Butch's leash was in one hand. Her chocolate cone was in the other.

Bobby looked over his shoulder.

Somebody watching might think they were a crazy parade. Another time it would be funny, but not today.

It was only a short block to the firehouse. The firehouse door was open. A big red fire truck was inside. A fireman was sitting outside reading a magazine.

"Excuse me," Mrs. Adams said with a gasp. "Have you seen a big, beautiful cat being chased by a dog?"

The fireman put down his magazine. "Why, yes," he said.

"When? How long ago? Which way were they headed?" Candy asked.

"Slow down," the fireman said. "It was maybe ten minutes ago. Those two went flying by."

"Did the cat look harmed?" Mrs. Adams demanded.

"She looked fine to me," the fireman replied. "She was leading that little dog on a merry chase."

"I believe the dog was chasing my cat," Mrs. Adams said stiffly.

The fireman grinned. "Maybe. But the cat looked like the one in charge."

"If my poor Ginger gets scared and runs up a tree," said Mrs. Adams, "I hope you'll bring a ladder and get her down."

"Okay, but I don't think Ginger was all that scared," the fireman said.

"But please, sir," Bobby asked, trying to sound bold, "where were they going?"

The fireman pointed. "They were running toward the baseball field."

Bobby thanked the fireman. "Let's go," he said.

The parade was off again. Bobby was

as fast as he could. Mrs. Agatha was running as fast as she could, wasn't very fast.

There was a small picnic area next to the ball field. A mom, a dad, and a set of twins about three years old were eating lunch at one of the picnic tables.

"Did you see a dog chasing a cat?" Bobby asked. Now he wasn't so afraid to speak up. He was close to finding Lucy.

"Doggie, doggie," the little boy yelled.

"Kitty, kitty," the little girl yelled back.

"Sshh," their father said.

Mrs. Agatha Adams looked like she was about to burst. "Did you see them?"

The mother nodded. "A little while ago. That orange cat almost knocked me over. A cute brown and white dog was after her."

"Lucy!" Bobby said.

"Ginger!" Mrs. Adams said.

Together they asked, "Which way did they go?"

"Toward the baseball diamond," the woman answered.

The parade was on the move again. Butch was pulling hard on his leash. Candy had dumped her ice cream cone. She needed both hands to control Butch. Shawn had tied his shoelaces at the fire station. He was running right next to Bobby. Mrs. Adams had a burst of energy. She was keeping up with the boys.

"There it is," Bobby shouted.

The baseball field was in sight. It looked like a Little League game was going on. There were parents in the stands. One team was in the field. The

had a player up at bat.

pulled ahead of the rest of the
He ran over to the baseball field.

He looked all around. "No Lucy," he
muttered.

Mrs. Agatha Adams came hurrying up.
Her hair was the color of an orange. Her
face was the color of a tomato.

"Do you see them?" she demanded.

Bobby shook his head. He looked
toward the batter's box.

The boy at bat took a swing at the ball
that was coming his way. It was a good
solid hit. The boy started running.

He wasn't the only one. A brown and
white beagle with black spots dashed out
from under the bleachers. She ran on the
field, too!

8
Play Ball!

"There's Lucy!" Bobby yelled.

"Where's Ginger?" Mrs. Adams yelled.

All the players were yelling, too. "Get that dog off the field!"

But Lucy knew what to do when she saw a ball go flying—chase it and bring it back. She ran past the pitcher's mound. She ran into left field. She was following that ball.

Just then, Bobby noticed a patch of orange under the stands. "Look, Mrs. Adams, it's Ginger," he said.

Ginger ran out on the field.

"Where's he going?" Mrs. Adams asked.

Shawn, Candy, and Butch joined them. "Lucy was chasing Ginger," Shawn said. "Now it looks like Ginger's chasing Lucy."

Sure enough, Ginger stayed right on Lucy's heels.

The teams were in an uproar. The umpire was yelling, "Who do those animals belong to?"

Uh-oh. Bobby was going to have to claim Lucy in front of all the baseball players, and the umpire, and the fans.

But before Bobby could say anything, Lucy found the ball. She picked it up. She looked around. Then she saw Bobby.

Lucy galloped over to him. She proudly dropped the ball at his feet. Then she lay down next to the ball. She was tired.

Ginger was still right behind Lucy. He took a long stretch. Then he lay down, too.

poor Ginger," Mrs. Adams
such a delicate kitty. I'm sure
been too much for him."

The umpire hurried up to them. "Are these animals yours?"

Mrs. Agatha Adams looked down at the umpire. "The cat is mine."

"That's my dog," Bobby said.

"Can you get them out of here?" the ump asked. "They're lying right on the baseline."

"Of course. Sweetie," Mrs. Adams called, "it's Mama. Wake up."

Ginger slowly opened his eyes. He took one look at Mrs. Adams and squeezed them shut.

"What about your dog, kid?" the ump asked.

By now, Lucy was snoring. Bobby shook

her lightly. "Fun's over, girl. Let's go home."

Lucy kept right on with her soft snores.

Bobby looked up. Most of the Little Leaguers and a few of the parents were milling around. Everyone was watching. He wished they would just go away. He pretended he was alone with Lucy.

"Come on, girl," he said. "Time to go."

Lucy wagged her tail. But she didn't wake up. Then Bobby had an idea.

"Shawn, do you still have those bones?"

Shawn handed over the bag of bones from Joe the butcher.

Bobby waved the bag in front of Lucy's nose. Lucy gave one huge yawn. Slowly, very slowly, she got up.

"That's it. Good dog," Bobby said. "I'll give you one of these to chew on later."

Lucy gave a happy bark.

All the baseball players clapped.

That woke up Ginger. "ME-OW!"

Bobby grabbed Lucy's collar. He didn't want the chase to start again. But Lucy didn't seem interested in running anymore.

Ginger didn't seem very interested, either. He started licking his paws.

Butch, on the other hand, was tugging on his leash. He wanted to see his pal, Lucy. And he was curious about that big orange-colored ball of fluff with a tail.

"I'm getting Butch out of here," Candy said. "Lucy and Ginger might be tired, but Butch isn't."

Candy pulled Butch away. "Come on, Butch. Maybe there will be some bones at home. Or if there aren't, I'll give you one of those cookies that look like bones. Or if we're out of those . . ."

"All right, show's over," the umpire said. "Everybody back to their positions."

Bobby felt so happy that without even thinking he said, "Thanks, everybody."

The players said things like, "No problem" and "So long, doggie."

Mrs. Adams picked up Ginger. He was a big load, but she didn't seem to mind. Ginger was so tired, he didn't even wiggle.

Lucy rubbed against Bobby's leg.

"I think Lucy wants to go home," Bobby told Shawn.

"I should think so," a familiar voice said. "I think it's time you came home, too."

Bobby didn't have to turn around to see who was speaking.

It was his mother.

9
Lost and Found

"Uh-oh," said Bobby under his breath.

His mother looked mad. Usually, Bobby could see his mother's dimples, even when she wasn't smiling. But not now.

"Bobby, what's going on?" Mrs. Quinn asked.

"Lucy ran away," Bobby started to explain.

"I know that much," his mother said. "I went to Shawn's house to find you. Ben told me that Lucy was gone. He gave me her leash." Mrs. Quinn pulled the leash out of her pocket and clipped it to Lucy's collar.

"She was lost," Bobby said quietly.

"Why didn't you come and get me?" Mrs. Quinn asked.

Bobby hung his head. "I wasn't watching Lucy the way I should. I was afraid you would be angry."

"Bobby was really, really worried about Lucy," Shawn told Mrs. Quinn.

"But I was really worried about Bobby. And you, too, Shawn," Mrs. Quinn said. "I didn't know where you went. I've been driving all over town looking for both of you."

"I thought we'd find Lucy a lot sooner," Bobby said. "I didn't think we would be gone so long."

"That's no excuse, Bobby, and you know it." But Mrs. Quinn reached over and gave Bobby a hug. She hugged Shawn, too. Then she hugged Lucy.

Mrs. Adams put down Ginger. As soon as he was on the ground, he stretched out. It was time for another catnap.

"I am Mrs. Agatha Adams." Mrs. Adams introduced herself to Bobby's mother. "And this is Ginger," she said, pointing to the sleeping cat.

"The cat that was in our yard!" Mrs. Quinn said.

"Lucy was chasing her," Bobby explained. "They took off together."

Lucy flopped down next to Ginger. Everybody was busy talking, and she was still tired.

"Your son was quite bold today," Mrs. Adams told Bobby's mother.

Bobby looked at Mrs. Adams. Him? Bold?

"Really?" Mrs. Quinn said faintly.

"Oh, yes," Mrs. Adams continued. "He went from place to place asking about Lucy. He would not rest until he knew Lucy was safe." Mrs. Adams turned to Bobby. "And because you kept looking, I found Ginger, too."

Mrs. Quinn looked at Bobby with surprise. "My goodness. You've had a very busy day."

Bobby was still a little surprised himself.

Lucy gave a small yip.

"Yes, so did you," Mrs. Quinn said to Lucy.

Mrs. Quinn said she would give Mrs. Adams and Ginger a ride home, and Shawn, of course.

That evening, Bobby had to tell his father what had happened.

Mrs. Quinn was making dinner. Lucy was asleep again, this time curled up on her blanket in the family room. Her favorite chewed-up slipper was under one paw. Mr. Quinn was sitting on the couch, ready to listen.

Bobby told him the whole story. He even told his father that he had snuck back to their house to look for Lucy. Bobby knew that's when he should have told his mother Lucy was gone.

After he had confessed everything, Bobby felt better. He felt almost as good as when he saw Lucy chasing the ball out to left field. But he had one more thing to say. "I'm really sorry, Dad."

"I know you are, Bobby," Mr. Quinn said. "But you see what can happen when you aren't paying attention."

Bobby nodded.

"Lucy was very lucky today," Mr. Quinn continued. "She could have gotten lost or hurt. Or worse."

Bobby didn't even want to think about Lucy not being lucky today. It was too horrible.

"And what about you?" asked his father. "Something bad might have happened to you. You know better than to go somewhere—anywhere—without asking your mother or me."

Bobby hung his head. "I know."

"You shouldn't have been running around town any more than Lucy. Even with a whole parade of people."

Bobby looked up at his father. "I'll never do anything like that again. I promise, Dad."

Lucy was awake. She'd heard her name. She got up and trotted over to Bobby.

Bobby picked up Lucy and put her on his lap. It felt so good to have her there. The best feeling in the world.

"I was going to punish you, Bobby," Mr. Quinn said. "But now that you've told me the whole story, I guess I won't."

Bobby was surprised. "Why not?"

"You were already punished. You had to worry about Lucy on the loose."

10
A Party

Bobby was having a party. It was a party for all his friends. It was one of the last days before school. Mrs. Quinn had set up the picnic table in the backyard. Mr. Quinn was grilling hamburgers and hot dogs.

Mr. Davis was sitting in a lawn chair talking to Candy. They were looking at Bobby and Shawn's drawings. There were new pictures of the Lone Ranger and Silver. Silver looked like a horse now, not a cow.

Bobby and Shawn were throwing a ball back and forth.

"Me, too! Me, too!" Ben yelled.

The boys took turns throwing the ball to Ben, too.

Lucy and Butch were playing their own game. They were both pulling on an old stuffed bear. They growled at each other, but it was only pretend growling.

"When are we going to eat?" Candy asked Mrs. Quinn.

"As soon as our special guests arrive."

Candy sat up straight. "Special guests? Who are they? Did you hire a clown? I love clowns. We had a clown at my birthday party when I was seven and—"

Mrs. Quinn laughed. "No, Candy. No clown."

Bobby stopped tossing the ball. "The guests are Mrs. Agatha Adams and Ginger."

Candy looked surprised. "Ginger! Ginger started all the trouble."

"It wasn't really Ginger's fault," Mrs. Quinn said. "Mrs. Adams and Ginger just moved to the neighborhood. Ginger got out of the house, and he didn't know how to get home."

Mr. Davis spoke up. "But what if Ginger and Lucy start chasing each other again?"

"Mrs. Adams was worried about that," Bobby's mother said, "but she told me she thinks she has solved the problem. She didn't say how."

Bobby flopped down on the grass. Shawn flopped down next to him.

"They can't go too far," Shawn said. "Not with your fenced yard. I wish I'd come over here the day Lucy got loose."

"I don't like to think about that day," Bobby said quietly.

"I know," Shawn said. "But Bobby, we did something good that day. You hate to talk to people you don't know. Me, too. But we talked to plenty of people that day."

Bobby had to smile. "There sure were lots of people. The kid in the park and the cashier in the store."

"And the people in line," Shawn added. "We talked to them, too."

"Joe the butcher," Bobby continued.

"And Mrs. Agatha Adams," Shawn said.

"Well, mostly she talked to us," Bobby pointed out.

Both boys grinned.

"We talked to that fireman," Bobby remembered.

"That was pretty brave," Shawn said.

"Absolutely," Bobby agreed.

"And the family at the picnic table," Shawn said.

"And we talked in front of two baseball teams," Bobby said. "And don't forget the ump."

Shawn nodded.

"We did it for Lucy," Bobby said.

"We weren't shy when it came to finding Lucy," said Shawn.

Bobby looked over at Lucy. She was still playing happily with Butch. "I have Lucy to thank for lots of things," Bobby said. "I'm not so shy anymore. I have friends." Bobby smiled at Shawn. He punched his arm. "Like you."

Shawn grinned right back. "Like me."

A noisy car pulled into the Quinns'

driveway. Mrs. Agatha Adams got out of the car. Her orange hair was piled on top of her head. She wore a dress covered in big gold stars. She wore long star-shaped earrings.

"Hello," she said. "Sorry I'm late."

Mrs. Quinn waved. "Didn't you bring Ginger?" she asked.

"Yes, I did."

Mrs. Adams went into the backseat. She lifted Ginger out and put him on the ground. Ginger was wearing something new. Around his neck was a collar. The collar was made of shiny stones that looked like diamonds. Attached to the collar was a gold leash.

Ginger didn't seem to mind being on a leash. He glided along like a small tiger. He looked very proud of himself.

Mrs. Adams looked proud of Ginger, too. She walked him into the yard.

Butch saw Ginger and barked. Ginger ignored him. Lucy didn't bark. She bounded right over.

"I guess Lucy remembers Ginger," Bobby said to Shawn.

Lucy certainly did. She stood in front of Ginger and gave one long howl.

Ginger had a greeting for Lucy, too. Ginger lifted his paw. He tapped Lucy on the chest. Cats can't smile. But Ginger sure looked like he was smiling.

"Lucy has a new friend," Shawn said.

Bobby laughed. "Humans, dogs, even cats. Everybody loves Lucy."

About the Author

For *Lucy on the Loose,* Ilene Cooper found inspiration right in her own house. Her cat, Homer, is always trying to run away. "If an unsuspecting deliveryman leaves the door open, Homer will dash out," Ilene says. "I considered buying a leash and a collar like Mrs. Agatha Adams, but I couldn't do it. Homer would have been too embarrassed."

Ilene Cooper has written many books for kids, including *Buddy Love—Now on Video, Choosing Sides,* and *Dead Sea Scrolls.* And of course, she also wrote the first book about Bobby and Lucy, *Absolutely Lucy.*